Amber McCarroll has published a romantic novel and a feature film script. She has also published two books on the healing arts, working with the inner significance of symbols. Amber's Gloriette is a small summerhouse set under a weeping willow tree in the corner of her garden. This is where she writes and finds her creative inspiration.

For the father of my children

First published in Great Britain in 2007 by
The Book Guild Ltd,
Pavilion View
19 New Road
Brighton, BN1 1UF

Typesetting in Talk to the Hand

Printed and bound in Thailand under the supervision of
MRM Graphics Ltd, Winslow, Buckinghamshire

A catalogue record for this book is available from
The British Library.

ISBN 978 1 84624 241 0

FAIRY TEATIME TALES

Book 1
Fairy Bergamot's New House

Amber McCarroll

Book Guild Publishing
Sussex, England

AMBER'S GLORIETTE
NEAR PIXIE GREEN
SUFFOLK
ENGLAND

FAIRY BERGAMOT'S NEW HOUSE

Dear Children,

I am writing to you from my Gloriette with news from the land of Faerie and as you will learn, whenever somebody pops by to see me from that land a new story is born. Well yesterday, I agreed to invite Fairy Bergamot to tea every Thursday when I am at home. In return, she has promised to keep me in touch with all the news from the land of Faerie so I will have a lot to tell whenever I write.

Fairy Bergamot has recently moved into the fairy
house next door to my Gloriette, at the base of the
willow tree. Since then she has spent her time
organizing the painting of it, inside and out. I asked
why she didn't just wave her magic wand. That's
when she told me she wanted her new house to look
rustic, – like one you would find in the country. As
she wasn't very good at creating 'rustic' with magic,
she has employed a very colourful tortoise named
Dockie to do the work for her.

When I first met Dockie, I couldn't believe my eyes. He was sitting beneath the willow tree smoking a pipe of wild lettuce herb; and you should really know that I can't abide smoking. Slung over one shoulder he had a large bag of scrolled paper that looked interesting. I was curious to know just exactly what these scrolls had on them – perhaps poems or paintings?

He must have guessed I was interested in the contents of his bag because he quickly volunteered that the scrolls were paintings of his life on the road. You see, Dockie is a gypsy; he carries his home firmly on his back everywhere he goes. He told me that he loves being on the road. Although it takes him for ever to get anywhere, he explained that he couldn't imagine a better way to live than travelling around the countryside, recording his adventures on scrolls of art paper. We chatted for a long while. Then I left him to his slow pace of work and went back into my Gloriette to get on with my own.

5

I'd just sat down at my desk when the most horrible thought flashed through my mind and quivered there unanswered: 'Don't gypsies eat hedgehogs?' I was almost sure I had read somewhere that hedgehogs are an old Romany delicacy. I was particularly concerned as I am responsible for a hedgehog named Horace. Let me tell you just how all this came about.

One morning a few weeks ago, I walked around to the back of my Gloriette only to find a mole busily pushing himself up in the middle of my blooming hollyhocks. You can imagine I was not amused. I called down to him in a very gruff voice, 'Stop it at once!' I might just as well have been talking to a brick wall for he paid me no attention. Well, I was so frustrated that I must have wished he would disappear because, as I turned around, there was Fairy Delphinium, resting on the edge of the tin bath where I grow my mint. You must always remember to be extra careful about what you wish for.

7
7

She spoke to me in such a sweet voice that I immediately felt a bit guilty about the tone I had used with the mole. However, I felt even worse when she politely informed me about the big assumption I had made. It turned out that the mole's name was Monsieur Taupe and had I spoken to him in his own language, he would certainly have answered. I apologized to him immediately in my best French. He was so charming that I fell quite in love with him. However, as I glanced down, I was quickly reminded of the damage he was causing to my hollyhocks. I decided, love him or not, he had to leave!

I was
thinking about
what to say next when Fairy Delphinium had a
brilliant idea. 'Monsieur Taupe would love the field
next to the paddock at your brother's house in Pixie
Green, where the rare bee orchids grow,' she
suggested, 'especially as the hens there lay lavender-
blue eggs'.

She continued by reminding me that my brother's
wife is a wonderful cook and was sure to invite
Monsieur Taupe to breakfast at least once a week,
and that they always ate brunch on Saturday when
they were at home. However, the icing on the cake
that finally won him over – as he had just arrived
from France and was tired of travelling – was
when he learned that my brother cooked brunch on
the barbecue, and
that his wife
always made
the best
blueberry
iced tea with
a special recipe
given to her by
Fairy Bergamot.

With everybody happy about this solution, Fairy Delphinium agreed to magically transport Monsieur Taupe straight to the field near Pixie Green so that he wouldn't even know he'd made the journey. However, there was one more thing that I had to do – remember, there is always a price to pay when you make a hasty wish. In return for ridding me of my mole problem, I had to be responsible for a hedgehog who had once been a broom head! Now, when I say be responsible, I mean I had to leave cat food out for him every night!

This all came about because a woman named Mrs Gillespie moved into a new home and inherited an old broom head that had been left outside the back door. During the day she had been so busy concentrating on moving in that she didn't even notice a broom head there. That evening, before going to her welcoming bed, she peeped outside the back door to see that everything was in order before locking up for the night. In the darkness she saw what She thought was a hedgehog. She ran into the kitchen and got some cat food. 'There, there, you sweet little hedgehog,' she said as she put down the food for him to eat.

The next day, when Mrs Gillespie got up and went outside in the morning light, she could see that it was just the head of an old broom. Angry with herself for being, as she saw it, a silly fool, she hurled the broom head to the end of her garden. And that's where Fairy Delphinium found him, crying his bristly eyes out and blowing his nose into a very dusty handkerchief.

Fairy Delphinium asked him why he was crying. He answered her in such a sad lost voice that her fairy heart went out to him, even though she was trying to plant delphinium seeds at the time. She vowed to help the poor little grubby broom head. He explained that when the purring sound of kindness in Mrs Gillespie's voice reached him over the cat food, he felt something that he had never felt before. He felt loved. It was such a wonderful feeling that he never wanted to be an old broom head ever again. He tried with all of his might to become a hedgehog, but something inside of him couldn't quite let go of the fact that he was a broom head. He lay there in his moment of glory knowing that the next morning the truth about his true identity would be revealed.

Fairy Delphinium made a hasty
spell but, like a hasty wish, it too
came with a price. Now she was left
with the responsibility of
putting cat food out
every night for the transformed
broom head, which she
named Horace the hedgehog.
Unless Horace was fed daily,
he would feel unloved.
Without love, he would
revert back to an old 'has
broom' and
fade away, and
poor Fairy
Delphinium
would have
failed in her role
as his fairy godmother.

So here I am – a stand-in godmother to one
Horace the hedgehog, with a gypsy painter, working
next door, who may enjoy hedgehog for his Sunday
lunch. What a mess! I ran outside to discuss this
with Dockie only to find him where I had left him;
smoking his smelly old pipe and still trying to decide
what to paint.

The good news is that Dockie is a vegetarian; the
bad news is he has decided to paint a picture of
my Gloriette. I asked him how long it would take.
'Oh at least two years,' he replied. I must say that
I was a little shocked at this news. I wondered
how long it had taken him to complete the scrolls
in his bag. As if reading my mind, he volunteered
that he had been working on them for over a
hundred years!

Then he mentioned
his love for
rocket, a special
tasty lettuce
that he could smell
growing in my kitchen
garden as we spoke.
'Do you think you could give
me some in exchange for
the painting?' he asked.
Knowing that rocket grows very quickly, I thought
this sounded like a very good idea. Dockie then
mentioned that if he had to go and get the rocket
himself, it would add another six months to the time
it took to finish the painting! I wasn't sure if he
was referring to Fairy Bergamot's house or the
picture of my Gloriette, however, I wasn't taking
any chances. I immediately suggested that Horace
could bring the rocket in his wheelbarrow to Dockie
every day, which would save him a lot of time.

Then Dockie said something that really pleased me.
'I am trying to give up smoking,' he said, smiling at
me sheepishly. 'I realize that it is a disgusting habit.
I find that chewing rocket leaves
helps me to break the habit of
putting my pipe in my mouth.'

So now you have the lie of
the land. Monsieur Taupe is given lavender-blue
eggs for breakfast three times a week and drinks
blueberry iced tea every Saturday at brunch. I feed
Horace cat food every night, and Horace supplies
Dockie with barrow loads of rocket. Then all is
calm and everyone is
happy. Dockie slowly paints,
taking his sweet time as he
constantly chews rocket
leaves while humming loud,
tuneless ditties into the ether.
He is quite a sight!

Yesterday I spied a piano accordion resting on a root of the willow tree where Dockie is painting. I fear that one day soon he may decide to serenade us all with some song from 'the old country'. So tomorrow, I am off to buy earplugs just in case.

Until the next time I write with news from my Gloriette, may your days be full of fairy magic. With love,

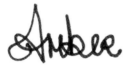

PS I hope you enjoy the *Fairy Information* that
follows. The fairies asked that I share these details
about their nature and ways with you.

FAIRY INFORMATION

Fairies are the guardians of Nature. Each fairy carries about her person the scent of the special plant that she protects. Fairy Bergamot smells of bergamot blossoms and fills my Gloriette with her scent whenever she comes to tea. Bergamot scent is said to help people to feel happy and lift dark shadows of sadness from their minds.

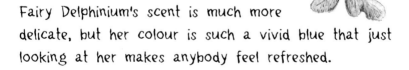

Fairy Delphinium's scent is much more delicate, but her colour is such a vivid blue that just looking at her makes anybody feel refreshed.

All fairies adore woody places, but it is the elves that love to hide in the ferns and have all the tree knowledge. It is said that gnomes live in caves, but even so, they are in charge of our gardens, especially the herb gardens where they love to sit on sunny afternoons.

Fairies can change size
at will; they can become
as small as the tiniest bee
and as large as a grown-
up. Fairy godmothers often
like to look like kind grandmothers
with wings. They are very
supportive of children who try
really hard to do their best.
That's why Fairy Delphinium
turned the broom head into
Horace the hedgehog, because
he had already tried very hard, all
by himself, to change from a grubby
old broom head into a
loveable hedgehog. So
remember, don't give
up when you find
things are difficult;
always believe in
yourself and the
fairies will appreciate
your efforts, even if you think
nobody else has noticed.

But the most important
thing the fairies
want me to share
with you is this:
if we don't look
after our green places,
the rare plants – like
the bee orchid found in
the paddock at Pixie Green,
now a favourite plant of Monsieur
Taupe's – will vanish.

However, even more
dreadful, – the fairies, who
protect those rare
plants, will also
disappear.

The land of Faerie depends on us to believe in all Nature's creatures. As Peter Pan tells us in Never Never Land, 'Every time somebody says "I don't believe in fairies", a fairy dies.'

So pay attention to all Nature's gifts that surround you. Believe in the magic of green places, and do your part to protect the planet's special plants and flowers that will soon vanish without your help. And know that every time you see a special flower like a bee orchid, it is a rare moment indeed... a bit like seeing a fairy.